This book belongs to:

_____

Good Morning, Garden

by
BARBARA BRENNER

illustrated by
DENISE ORTAKALES

NORTHWORD PRESS
Chanhassen, Minnesota

The illustrations were created using various types of sculpted papers
The text and display type were set in Novarese and Improv Inline
Composed in the United States of America
Designed by Lois A. Rainwater
Edited by Aimee Jackson

Books for Young Readers
NorthWord Press
18705 Lake Drive East
Chanhassen, MN 55317
www.northwordpress.com

Library of Congress Cataloging-in-Publication Data

Brenner, Barbara.
Good morning, garden / by Barbara Brenner ; illustrated by Denise Ortakales.
p.   cm.
Summary: Upon entering a garden one morning, a child greets the flowers, plants, insects, and animals there.
ISBN 1-55971-888-9 (hc)
[1. Gardens—Fiction. 2. Morning—Fiction. 3. Stories in rhyme.] I. Ortakales, Denise, ill. II. Title.

PZ8.3.B745Go 2004

[E]—dc22   2003054195

Printed in Singapore
10 9 8 7 6 5 4 3 2 1

Good morning, sun.
Good morning, sky.

Good morning,
orange butterfly
drinking dew.

Good morning, blue
delphinium,
purple phlox,
pink hollyhocks.

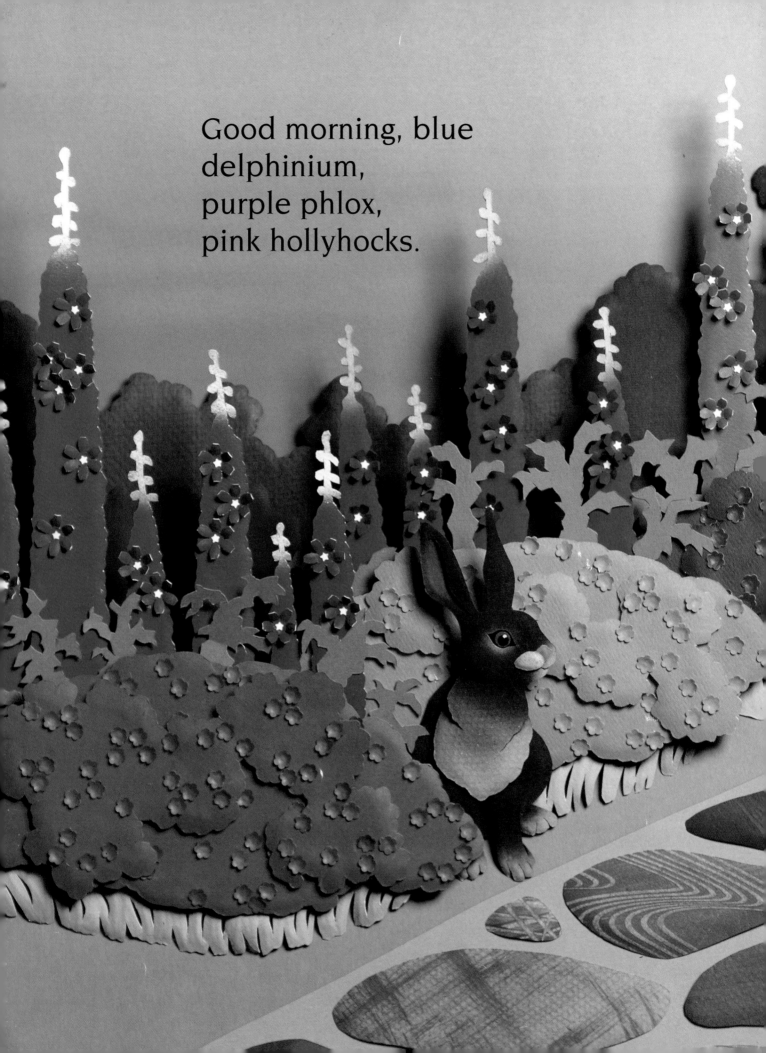

Good morning, bee balm
and bumblebees.

Good morning, cherries
on cherry trees,

and blackberries
on bushes.

Good morning to plants
with funny names.
Cow Vetch.
Goat's Beard.

Sneezeweed.
Dogbane.

And don't forget
Forget-me-not.

Good morning, toad
under my flowerpot,

garter snake
among the leaves,

swallows nesting
in the eaves,

chipmunk sitting
by his hole,

mole,

spiders
and ladybugs,
dragonflies
and
even slugs!

To all living things
in this place…

Good morning!

Photograph by Sasha Zhitneva

BARBARA BRENNER is an award-winning author who has written more than eighty books for children and a dozen non-fiction books for adults. Her book *On the Frontier With Mr. Audubon* is on the Master List of the William Allen White Award Books and was selected by School Library Journal as "The Best of the Best" among the books published for children throughout twenty-six publishing seasons. Ms. Brenner has won the ALA's Notable Book Award for *Wagon Wheels*, *Snake-Lover's Diary*, and *Voices: Poetry and Art from Around the World*, which was also an ALA Best Book for YA in 2000. *Wagon Wheels* was also a nominee for the William Allen White Award and is a Reading Rainbow selection, as is *The Tremendous Tree Book*. *The Falcon Sting* was a candidate for the Edgar Allen Poe Award given by the Mystery Writers of America. In 1986, Ms. Brenner was elected Distinguished Pennsylvania Author of the Year. She lives in Pennsylvania with her husband, Fred.

DENISE ORTAKALES is a graduate of The Art Institute of Boston. Her award-winning paper sculptures have appeared in consumer and business magazines, as well as children's magazines and books, including *Planets* and *Carrot in My Pocket*. Denise is a life-long resident of Laconia, New Hampshire, where she lives with her husband and two sons. You can see more of her work at her Web site, www.sculptedpaper.com.